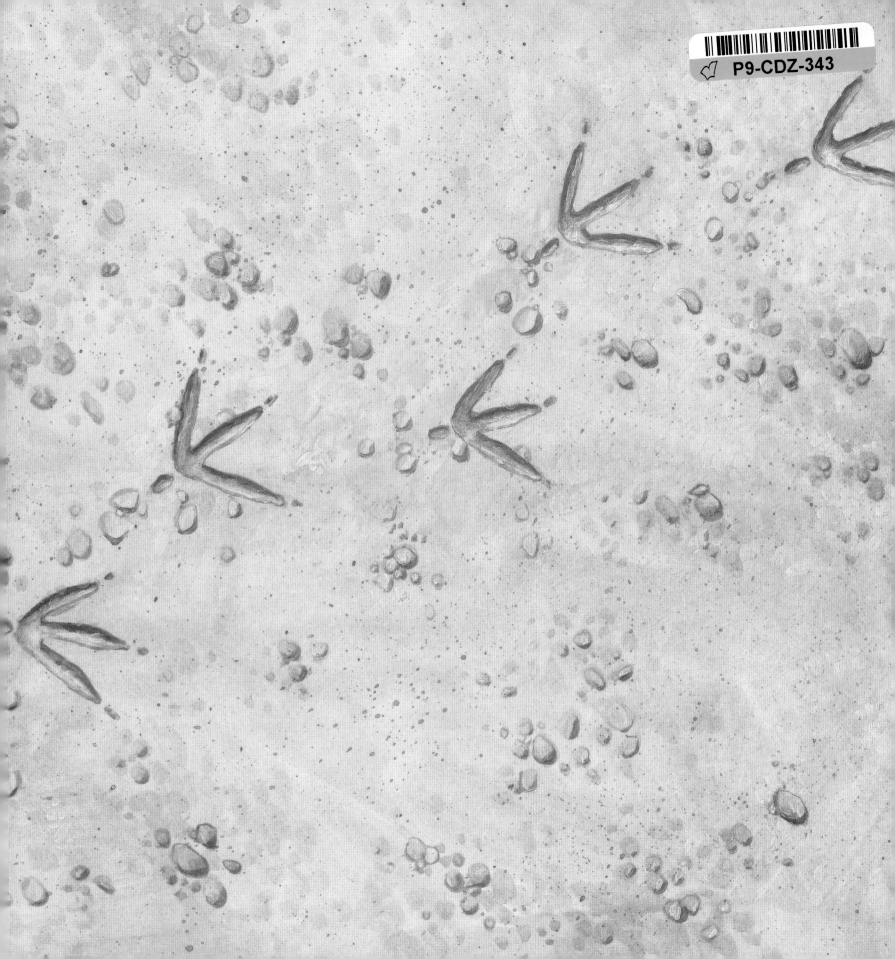

Acoustic Rooster

and His Barnyard Band

Kwame Alexander
Illustrated by Tim Bowers

PUBLISHED BY SLEEPING BEAR PRESS

Acoustic Rooster sat outside
strumming his bass guitar.
He practiced jazz all summer long
so he could be a star.

Now every year about this time,
Farmer announced his plan
to hold a Barnyard Talent Show
and find the farm's best band.

Acoustic Rooster asked to join
Thelonious Monkey's crew.
But Farmer's rules prevented that
because they lived at the Zoo.

Mules Davis led an orchestra
that featured three cool cats.

Ella Finchgerald had a trio
but Rooster couldn't scat.

Rooster was feeling kind of blue,
then heard a baby grand.
"I have a great idea," he said.
"I'll start my own jazz band."

So, he went to see his cousin,
a pianist of great fame.
He found him on the riverbank.
Duck Ellington's his name.

Duck took him to the Cotton Club
to hear Bee Holiday sing.
Bee said, "Honey, I'll join your band,
as long as you can swing."

A drummer with a big ol' smile
was itching for a gig.
"I've got cowbells and conga drums.
I'm a percussion pig."

"Mighty fine to meet you," said Pig.
"I'm Poncho Ernesto Cruz."

Duck told him, "Friend, your name's too long.
Pork Chop is what we'll use."

The talent show began with Mules blowing his bebop horn.

Then Ella followed with a song
as sweet as candy corn.

Acoustic Rooster's band performed
a bossa nova tune.
"The Hen from Ipanema" made
the barnyard chickies swoon.

The band's encore came 'round midnight
in grand finale style.

Acoustic Rooster's jazzy riff
drove the barnyard wild.

When at last the votes were tallied,
Mules Davis won first prize.
Rooster and his band placed second,
and tears swam in his eyes.

"We really got some buzz," Bee said,
then Mules headed their way.
The words he spoke brought lots of smiles:

Acoustic Rooster headed home,
his guitar in his hand.
He didn't win the talent show,
but he had the **world's best band.**

Acoustic Rooster's Jazz Glossary

Jazz is a form of American music that started in African American communities in the early 1900s. It combines European and African musical traditions to create a sound that uses multiple rhythms, improvisation, and syncopation. Jazz has many styles, such as New Orleans Dixieland, big-band-style swing, bebop, and a variety of Latin jazz and fusion.

Musical Vocabulary

Acoustic Music
Music that is produced by instruments whose sound is created without the aid of electricity.

Baby Grand
A small version of the grand piano.

Bass Guitar
A four- or five-string instrument with steel strings that produces a low sound.

Bebop
A style of instrumental jazz that features a fast tempo and a lot of improvisation. It's also known as bop.

Bossa Nova
A style of cool jazz developed in Brazil in 1956 by João Gilberto.

Conga Drum
A tall, slender, Cuban drum that originated in Africa.

Cowbell
A hand percussion instrument named after the bell used by farmers to keep track of their cows.

Gig
Another name for a musical performance.

Percussion Instrument
An object that produces sound by being hit, shaken, rubbed, or scraped.

Riff
A repeated phrase or pattern in jazz music, often used during a solo performance.

Scat
Vocals made up of random sounds and syllables sung to melodies and rhythms.

Strumming
Stroking the strings of a guitar with the fingers or flat pick.

Swing
A form of jazz music developed in the 1930s that uses a rhythm and groove that people can dance to.

Musicians, Characters, and Music

Bee Holiday is based on Billie Holiday, who was an American jazz singer and songwriter. She was admired all over the world for her deeply personal and intimate singing style.

Ella Finchgerald is based on Ella Jane Fitzgerald, an American jazz vocalist, known for her improvisation and scat singing. She is widely considered the greatest jazz singer of all time.

Duck Ellington is based on Edward Kennedy "Duke" Ellington, an American pianist, composer, big-band leader, and one of the greatest figures in the history of jazz.

Mules Davis is based on Miles Dewey Davis III, an American jazz trumpeter, flugelhorn player, bandleader, composer, and one of the most influential musicians of the twentieth century.

Thelonious Monkey is based on Thelonious Sphere Monk, an American jazz pianist and composer often regarded as a founder of the bebop style of jazz.

"The Hen from Ipanema" is based on the well-known bossa nova song "The Girl from Ipanema," a worldwide hit of the 1960s written by Brazilian musicians Antonio Carlos Jobim and Vinicius de Moraes.

"Kind of Blue," an album by trumpeter Miles Davis is probably considered the best-selling jazz record of all time.

"As Long As You Can Swing," is inspired by Duke Ellington's hit song, "It Don't Mean a Thing (If It Ain't Got That Swing)."

"'Round Midnight" is a 1944 jazz standard by pianist Thelonious Monk. It is the most-recorded jazz standard composed by a jazz musician.

The Cotton Club was a famous jazz night club founded in the 1920s in Harlem, New York. The club helped launch the careers of jazz greats Fletcher Henderson, Cab Calloway, and Duke Ellington, whose orchestra was the club's house band from 1927 to 1931.

Acoustic Rooster's Jazz Timeline

1700s
Powerful rhythms of African percussion, slaves' work songs, and spiritual hymns form the roots of the American music genre that would become known as jazz.

1800s
With the emigration of many Europeans to America, new musical traditions arrive in our cities and ports. African American composer Scott Joplin combines European music styles with spiritual and work songs to create ragtime.

1900s
New Orleans is a city filled with many different cultures. African American musicians like King Oliver's Creole Jazz Band merge these European musical influences with blues, ragtime, marching band music, and other elements to create a new style of music known as jazz.

1920s
As African Americans migrate to northern cities like Chicago and New York, they bring jazz with them. Jazz musicians like Louis Armstrong and Duke Ellington are heard on America's radio airwaves as well as in dance halls.

1930s
During the Great Depression, jazz helps people escape the hardships of the time. Musicians like Fletcher Henderson, Glenn Miller, and Benny Goodman create a new style of jazz called big-band swing, which people can dance to. Jazz singers like Billie Holiday and Ella Fitzgerald emerge during this era.

1940s
Musicians like Dizzy Gillespie, Charlie Bird Parker, and Billy Eckstine help jazz shift from danceable and popular swing music toward a more challenging and much faster form called bebop.

1950s

Cool jazz emerges, with its calm, smooth sounds performed by artists like Dave Brubeck. An extension of bebop, known as hard bop, incorporating rhythm and blues, gospel, and the blues, is perfected by Miles Davis, Art Blakey and the Jazz Messengers, and Thelonious Monk.

1960s

During this decade of rapid change and unrest in American life, Martin Luther King Jr. makes his famous "I Have a Dream" speech to encourage equality for people of all races. The civil rights movement has a major impact on jazz. Many artists express their anger and disappointment at the slow pace of change through jazz music. These free jazz artists—Ornette Coleman, Cecil Taylor, John Coltrane, Sonny Rollins, and Sun Ra—abandon most traditional jazz conventions and create a new highly experimental form of music.

1970s

The integration of funk, soul, and rhythm and blues music into jazz results in the creation of jazz-funk, popularized by musicians like the great Herbie Hancock.

1980s –1990s

A commercial form of jazz fusion called smooth jazz becomes successful with the advent of saxophonists like Grover Washington Jr., Kirk Whalum, and Boney James. In the 1990s, acid jazz, influenced by jazz funk and electronic dance music, is developed in England, with Roy Ayers and Donald Byrd leading the way.

2000s

In 2004, Wynton Marsalis, who has been creating music in the tradition of such jazz pioneers as Louis Armstrong and Duke Ellington for more than two decades, becomes artistic director of Jazz at Lincoln Center in New York City.

For Deanna, AJ, Lesléa, and my favorite jazz vocalist on earth, Titilayo.
—K. A.

To Tom Carroll
—T. B.

Text Copyright © 2011 Kwame Alexander
Illustration Copyright © 2011 Tim Bowers

Sleeping Bear Press™

315 East Eisenhower Parkway, Suite 200
Ann Arbor, MI 48108
www.sleepingbearpress.com

Printed and bound in the United States.

10 9 8 7 6 5 4

Library of Congress Cataloging-in-Publication Data

Alexander, Kwame.
Acoustic Rooster and his barnyard band / written by Kwame Alexander ;
illustrated by Tim Bowers.
p. cm.
Summary: Acoustic Rooster forms a jazz band with Duck Ellington, Bee Holliday, and Pepe Ernesto Cruz
to compete in the annual Barnyard Talent Show against such greats as Thelonious Monkey, Mules Davis, and Ella Finchgerald.
Includes glossary, notes on the characters and songs, and jazz timeline.
ISBN 978-1-58536-688-0
[1. Stories in rhyme. 2. Musicians--Fiction. 3. Jazz--Fiction. 4. Domestic animals--Fiction. 5. Contests--Fiction.] I. Bowers, Tim, ill. II. Title.
PZ8.3.A3757Aco 2011
[E]--dc22
2010053709